FATED

BY

THE CURSE

A Shifter's Rejected Destiny

Tessa Wildwind

Copyright Page

CONTENTS

CHAPTER 1

The Chase

Freedom. It was the cruelest illusion. No matter how far Aria Bennett ran, it always stayed just beyond her grasp. Her lungs burned, her heartbeat a frantic drum as she darted through the shadowed alley, the damp scent of rain clinging to her skin. Behind her, a low growl rippled through the air, rich with menace.

"Stop!" The alpha's voice sliced through the night, sharp and unyielding. "Unregistered shifters are a danger to everyone."

The command rolled over her like a thunderclap, heavy with dominance, but Aria gritted her teeth and pushed forward. Her wolf whimpered under the weight of his power, but Aria forced it down. She didn't have time to wrestle with instincts when survival was on the line.

The ladder loomed ahead, bolted to the crumbling brick wall like an invitation to escape. Her fingers wrapped around the cold rungs, trembling with adrenaline as she hauled herself upward. A glance down revealed the alpha rounding the corner, his golden eyes catching the faint glow of a flickering streetlamp.

"You're only making this harder on yourself," he growled, his voice roughened with anger. "Stop running, rogue!"

"Not today," she muttered under her breath.

Her claws extended instinctively as she scrambled onto the balcony. One swift swipe severed the rope holding the ladder, sending it clattering to the ground below. The noise echoed through the alley like a gunshot, and Aria didn't wait to see how close the alpha was. Seconds could mean the difference between freedom and being dragged back to Golden Claw City.

Her boots hit the pavement with a muffled thud as she dropped into another alley. The narrow corridor smelled of damp earth, rusted metal, and old oil. She forced herself to keep moving, her chest tight with the strain of running. The weight of the alpha's pursuit pressed against her, relentless as a predator closing in on its prey.

"I don't want to hurt you," his voice carried through the darkness, a growl layered beneath the words. "But I will if you force my hand."

The lie was almost laughable. Alphas like him didn't ask — they took. The memory of her mother's face, gaunt with exhaustion and fear, flashed in her mind. Aria's resolve hardened. She wouldn't let them cage her the way they had her mother.

The tarp-covered shape of her bike came into view, hidden behind a dumpster at the edge of the parking lot. Relief surged in her chest. Her Yamaha YZF-R6 wasn't just a machine — it was her lifeline, her way out.

She tore off the cover, revealing the sleek black frame beneath. Swinging her leg over, she jammed the key into the ignition, her fingers trembling with urgency. The engine roared to life, shattering the stillness.

The alpha emerged from the shadows, his towering frame backlit by the faint glow of a streetlamp. His golden eyes burned with an intensity that made her stomach clench. A faint scar sliced across his jawline, giving his otherwise commanding presence a rugged edge.

"Stay," he ordered, his voice a low rumble that sent vibrations through the air. It wasn't a suggestion — it was a command wrapped in raw power.

Her wolf hesitated, caught in the magnetic pull of his dominance. For a moment, she felt the weight of his will pressing against hers, like a tide threatening to pull her under. But Aria gripped the handlebars tighter, her knuckles turning white. "Not happening."

The alpha's lips curled into a dangerous smile. "You can't outrun me, little rogue. You're wasting your time."

"Good thing I don't mind wasting yours." She twisted the throttle, the tires screeching as the bike shot forward.

The city blurred into a streak of neon lights and shadow as Aria tore through the streets. The wind howled against her face, tangling her hair in a wild mess. Behind her, the alpha's growl echoed faintly, a reminder that the chase wasn't over.

Her wolf stirred uneasily, a low growl rumbling in her chest. *He's strong. Too strong.*

"I know," Aria muttered, her voice barely audible over the roar of the bike. "But he's not catching us."

Golden Claw City was a death sentence for someone like her. Omegas weren't safe there—they were controlled, exploited, broken. Her mother's fate was proof enough of that. And Aria had no intention of becoming anyone's pawn.

The highway stretched ahead, dark and empty, a ribbon of asphalt that felt like freedom. The city lights faded into the distance, swallowed by the inky blackness of the night. Aria's pulse began to steady, the adrenaline still humming in her veins.

Her eyes flicked to the mirror. A pair of faint headlights glimmered far behind, too distant to follow yet close enough to haunt. She gritted her teeth and pressed the throttle harder.

The chase wasn't over. It never was.

CHAPTER 2

The Marked

The open road was a reprieve, but it wasn't freedom. Not really. Aria Bennett tightened her grip on the bike's handlebars, her pulse a frantic drumbeat in her ears. The distant hum of her pursuer's engine had faded, swallowed by the night, but her wolf's restless growl warned her not to relax.

Golden Claw alphas didn't quit. Especially not ones like him—scarred, calculating, and commanding dominance like it was woven into his very essence.

She veered off the highway onto a winding dirt path that cut through the forest. The towering pines loomed overhead, their darkened branches clawing at the sky. Here, among the trees, was where she felt safest. The wilds didn't care about pack laws or shifter politics. Out here, instincts ruled.

Killing the engine, she let silence envelop her. Swinging her leg off the bike, she grabbed her pack and disappeared into the shadows. Her steps were soft, deliberate, every crunch of gravel underfoot a reminder of how exposed she was. She found a clearing and set to work, her movements quick and efficient.

THE CAMP

The firepit had long been abandoned, overgrown with weeds and encircled by fallen branches. Aria knelt, clearing a small patch of earth. A few strikes from her flint brought the kindling to life, and a weak flame flickered to life, casting its glow against the encroaching darkness.

She pulled an energy bar from her pack and ripped it open. It wasn't much, but it would keep her going. The first bite tasted like cardboard, but she forced it down.

Her mind, however, was anything but quiet. The alpha's golden eyes haunted her thoughts, his words still echoing in her ears. *"Stop running, rogue."*

But it wasn't just his pursuit that bothered her — it was his presence. The way his dominance had rippled through the air like a living thing, pressing against her wolf, leaving an invisible mark she couldn't shake.

You're marked, her wolf whispered, its voice soft and urgent.

Her grip tightened around the energy bar, crumpling the wrapper. "Shut up," she hissed under her breath. But her wolf was right. The alpha had done more than chase her; he'd left an imprint, a tether she couldn't sever.

Her mother's voice echoed in her mind, distant and bitter: *Alphas always find what they claim.*

Aria's stomach twisted, nausea threatening to rise. "He hasn't claimed me," she muttered fiercely. "He never will." The words were defiance wrapped in desperation, a shield against the growing storm inside her.

A THREAT LURKING

The fire crackled softly, its warmth doing little to thaw the icy pit in her stomach. She leaned back against a fallen log, her body aching from the hours of running. The forest was still, but her wolf stirred uneasily, its growl a low vibration just beneath her skin.

A twig snapped.

The sound was faint, but it cut through the night like a gunshot. Aria was on her feet in an instant, claws extending as her wolf surged to the surface.

"Relax," a voice drawled, smooth and rich with an edge of steel.

The alpha stepped into the firelight, his golden eyes gleaming with the same intensity that had haunted her. His scar caught the flickering glow, the jagged line deepening the shadows of his face. His presence was a weight that filled the clearing, oppressive and magnetic all at once.

"How?" The question slipped out before she could stop it. She'd been careful—no trail, no scent markers. He shouldn't have been able to follow her.

He smiled, slow and deliberate, a predator savoring its prey. "You're not as invisible as you think, little rogue. Defiance has its own scent, and yours is impossible to miss."

Her wolf whimpered, but Aria clenched her fists, planting her feet firmly. "Turn around and walk away, Alpha. You're not welcome here."

His smile widened, amusement flickering in his eyes. "You don't scare me."

"Good," she snapped. "I'm not trying to scare you. I'm trying to save you."

That earned her a chuckle, low and dark. "Save me? From what?"

"From me," she growled, her claws twitching.

He didn't flinch. Instead, he took a deliberate step closer, his gaze never leaving hers. "You've been running for a long time, haven't you? Tell me, Aria—how does it feel to always look over your shoulder?"

The question hit harder than she wanted to admit. Her lips parted, but no answer came. Instead, her wolf rose again, a restless energy prickling along her skin. She forced it down, her voice sharp. "What do you want?"

His expression darkened, the playful edge fading. "Golden Claw doesn't waste resources on rogues," he said evenly. "If I wanted you dead, you wouldn't have made it out of Jacksonville."

The statement hung heavy in the air, chilling her despite the fire's warmth. He wasn't here to kill her. That much was clear.

"Then why?" she demanded.

"Because you're more dangerous than you realize," he said, his tone dropping lower. "And I'm not the only one hunting you."

CHAPTER END

The alpha's words struck like a hammer, cracking the walls she'd spent years building around herself. She wasn't just running anymore—she was prey in a game she didn't understand.

And the real danger was still out there.

CHAPTER 3

The Bond's Weight

The fire crackled between them, a faint buffer against the tension that filled the clearing. Aria Bennett stood motionless, her claws still extended, her wolf bristling beneath her skin. The alpha didn't advance further, but his presence remained oppressive, his golden eyes pinning her in place.

"More dangerous than I realize?" Aria finally said, breaking the silence. Her voice dripped with sarcasm, masking the flicker of unease she couldn't shake. "That's a bold statement coming from someone who chased me across state lines."

His lips quirked, not quite a smile, but close. "I didn't say it was your fault."

"Fault or not, I didn't ask for your opinion," she shot back.

The alpha tilted his head, studying her like she was some fascinating puzzle he couldn't quite solve. "You think running makes you safe," he said, his tone low and deliberate. "You think it makes you invisible. But you're leaving footprints, Aria. And there are those out there far less... considerate than me."

Her wolf stirred at his words, but Aria clenched her jaw, forcing the unease back down. "So, what? You're here to save me?" She laughed, the sound sharp and humorless. "I don't need saving, and I definitely don't need you."

His expression darkened, the faint amusement in his eyes replaced by something harder. "You might not want me, but you need me. Whether you like it or not."

Aria crossed her arms, claws retracting as she took a step closer to the fire, her defiance burning as bright as the flames. "Let's skip the cryptic alpha routine, shall we? What's coming for me? And why do you care?"

THE WARNING

The alpha's gaze never wavered, the flickering firelight casting sharp shadows across his face. "Do you know what makes omegas special?" he asked instead, his voice carrying the weight of something ancient.

Her stomach tightened. "They're rare," she said, her tone dismissive. "Special enough to get hunted down like trophies."

"They're more than rare," he corrected, his golden eyes narrowing. "They're anchors. Stabilizers. Packs thrive because of them, their bonds strengthened, their instincts balanced. Without omegas, alphas descend into chaos. You think running keeps you safe, but all it's done is make you a beacon."

The words settled heavily over her, and Aria's pulse quickened despite herself. "Beacon for what?" she demanded, though she wasn't sure she wanted to hear the answer.

"Power," he said simply. "Rogues like you are dangerous because you're unbound. You don't belong to a pack, and that makes you... unstable. Alphas want to claim you because your strength feeds theirs. But it's not just alphas you should worry about."

Aria's breath hitched, her fingers curling into fists. "What else is there?"

"**The Old Ones.**" His voice dipped lower, the words almost reverent. "They're waking, and they're hungry. You've heard the stories."

"Fairy tales," she scoffed, but her wolf stirred uneasily.

"You think this is a game?" He leaned forward, his golden eyes blazing. "I didn't track you because I wanted to. I did it because if I didn't, they would."

ARIA'S DEFIANCE

The fire popped loudly, a spark leaping into the air before fading into the night. Aria's mind raced, the weight of his words pressing against the thin walls she'd built around herself. Old Ones? Anchors? None of this mattered. What mattered was staying free.

"**And what's your plan?**" she asked, her tone sharper now. "Drag me back to Golden Claw City, slap a collar on me, and call it a day?"

The alpha's jaw tightened, a muscle ticking just beneath the surface. "You really think that's what this is about?"

"I think it's always about control," she said coldly. "Alphas want omegas because we're convenient. Because we're easy to use."

"Easy?" He laughed then, the sound low and dangerous. "There's nothing easy about you, Aria."

The way he said her name sent a shiver down her spine, but she refused to let it show. "You don't know me."

"I know enough." His gaze softened, though his posture remained rigid. "I know you're stubborn. Reckless. And brave, even when you shouldn't be. But I also know you're exhausted, and you're not going to win this fight alone."

Her throat tightened at his words. She hated that he could see through her so easily, that he could strip away her defenses with a few simple observations. But she wouldn't let him break her. Not now. Not ever.

"I've been fine on my own," she said, her voice quiet but firm.

"For now," he said softly. "But the storm's coming, little rogue. And when it hits, you'll have two choices — run and die, or stand and fight."

<hr>

CHAPTER END

The alpha stood, his towering frame cutting a shadow against the firelight. "You don't have to trust me, Aria. But you should trust this — I'm not your enemy."

She didn't respond, her jaw set as she watched him turn and melt back into the shadows. The fire crackled faintly in his absence, but the cold crept in anyway, wrapping around her like a vice.

Her wolf growled low, uneasy. And for the first time in years, Aria felt it too.

The storm was coming. And no amount of running would save her from it.

CHAPTER 4

Shadows Stirring

The fire had burned down to embers, its warmth barely cutting through the chill that seeped into Aria Bennett's bones. She stared at the faint orange glow, her mind racing in circles around the alpha's words.

The storm's coming, little rogue.

Her wolf growled softly, uneasy. She hated that part of herself—the way it always reacted to dominance, to warnings. But this time, even Aria couldn't entirely dismiss the gnawing sense of dread curling in her gut.

She stood and kicked dirt over the fire, extinguishing the last of the embers. The darkness swallowed her, the forest eerily quiet save for the rustling of leaves in the wind. Clutching her pack, she moved through the trees, her steps soft and deliberate. She didn't know where she was going. She just knew she couldn't stay.

SIGNS OF THE STORM

The night felt different—heavier. The air carried a strange hum, faint and almost imperceptible, but it prickled against Aria's skin like static. Her wolf whined, the sound low and nervous.

"Get it together," she muttered under her breath. But her words sounded hollow even to her own ears.

The forest opened into a clearing, bathed in the silver light of the moon. Aria paused, her instincts screaming at her to turn back. The clearing felt wrong. The trees around its edges seemed to lean inward, their branches clawing toward the center like skeletal hands. The hum in the air grew louder, vibrating through her chest.

And then she saw it—a shadow that wasn't cast by the moonlight, moving against the far edge of the clearing.

Aria's breath caught, her claws extending instinctively. The shadow shifted, elongating, its edges fraying like smoke. She crouched low, her heart hammering in her chest. Her wolf snarled, pushing at her skin, but she forced it down. Whatever this was, it wasn't natural.

The shadow stopped moving, coiling into itself. A pair of faint, glowing red eyes blinked open, and a low, guttural sound filled the air — a noise that wasn't quite a growl but resonated with the weight of something ancient.

Aria froze. Every instinct screamed at her to run, but she couldn't move, her legs locked in place. The thing in the clearing shifted again, the red eyes narrowing. It was watching her.

AN UNLIKELY RESCUE

A sudden roar shattered the tension, the sound tearing through the stillness like thunder. The shadow recoiled, its form twisting violently before dissolving into the air like smoke caught in a gale.

Aria stumbled back, her breath coming in ragged gasps as a familiar scent hit her — earthy, sharp, and undeniably alpha.

He emerged from the trees, his golden eyes blazing. "Are you trying to get yourself killed?"

Aria glared at him, forcing her legs to steady beneath her. "I didn't ask for your help."

"And yet, here I am," he said, his tone clipped as he scanned the clearing. "You shouldn't be here."

"I didn't realize I needed a permission slip," she shot back, though her voice lacked its usual bite. The encounter had rattled her more than she wanted to admit.

The alpha turned to her, his expression hard. "That wasn't a shifter. It wasn't even alive."

She crossed her arms, trying to suppress the shiver crawling up her spine. "Then what was it?"

"One of the Old Ones' shadows," he said grimly. "A scout. They're drawn to power, to weakness, to anything that feels like prey."

Her stomach twisted, the memory of those glowing red eyes burning in her mind. "It wasn't hunting me."

He stepped closer, his golden gaze locking onto hers. "No, it was claiming you."

A FRAGILE ALLIANCE

The words hit like a blow, stealing the air from her lungs. "Claiming me? What does that even mean?"

The alpha's jaw tightened, a muscle ticking beneath his scar. "It means they've marked you. You've been running for so long, you've left a trail even they can follow. And now that they've found you, they won't stop."

Her pulse thundered in her ears. "Why me?"

"You know why," he said softly, the edge in his voice softening. "You're an omega, Aria. And you're unbound. That makes you a beacon for power, for chaos."

She swallowed hard, her claws retracting as her hands fell to her sides. "So what now? You drag me back to your pack, make me your problem?"

His lips curved into a faint, humorless smile. "You already are my problem."

Aria's wolf growled, a low, uncertain sound. She hated the way his words felt like truth, hated the way her body betrayed her with that faint pull toward him. "I don't need your help."

"You don't have a choice anymore," he said bluntly. "They've marked you, Aria. You're in this whether you like it or not."

She stared at him, her mind racing. She didn't trust him. She couldn't. But the memory of those red eyes, of that thing in the clearing, made her doubt her ability to survive this alone.

"Fine," she said finally, the word heavy with reluctance. "But this doesn't mean I trust you."

The alpha inclined his head, his golden eyes gleaming with something that almost looked like approval. "Good. I don't need you to trust me. I just need you to stay alive."

CHAPTER END

The forest fell silent again as they moved, the weight of the alpha's presence pressing against Aria's every step. Her wolf whined softly, a mix of fear and something she refused to name.

The shadows around them seemed deeper now, the hum in the air faint but ever-present. Aria's jaw tightened as she glanced at the alpha beside her.

The storm was no longer coming. It was **here.**

CHAPTER 5

The forest was alive with whispers. Not the natural sounds of rustling leaves or the occasional cry of an owl—this was something deeper, older, and far more unnerving. Aria Bennett could feel it thrumming through her veins as she moved, her every step shadowed by the alpha's looming presence.

Her wolf was restless, pacing just beneath the surface. *You shouldn't trust him.* It growled, a quiet warning. But trust was the last thing on Aria's mind. Right now, survival was all that mattered.

"Do you always walk this slow?" she asked, breaking the heavy silence. Her tone was sharp, masking the unease prickling at the edges of her mind.

The alpha, who still hadn't given her his name, shot her a sidelong glance. "Do you always talk this much?"

Aria scowled. "Just trying to fill the awkward silence. Wouldn't want you to feel lonely."

A faint smirk tugged at his lips, but it disappeared as quickly as it came. "We're close."

"Close to what?" she demanded, her claws twitching at her sides.

He didn't answer. Instead, he stopped abruptly, his golden eyes scanning the darkened woods. Aria followed his gaze, her stomach tightening as the faint hum she'd felt earlier returned, louder now. The air secmed to ripple around them, charged with an unnatural energy.

THE WARNING SIGNS

The alpha's posture stiffened, every muscle in his body coiled like a spring. "Stay close."

Aria bristled. "I can handle myself."

"This isn't about you, rogue," he said sharply, his gaze never leaving the trees. "It's about them."

Before she could respond, a sound split the air—a guttural, bone-deep vibration that made her skin crawl. It wasn't a growl, but something far more primal, like the earth itself was groaning in protest. The shadows around them seemed to thicken, stretching and writhing unnaturally.

"Run," the alpha ordered, his voice low and deadly.

Aria hesitated for only a second before her instincts kicked in. She turned and sprinted, her wolf surging to the surface, lending her speed. Behind her, she heard the alpha roar, a sound so fierce it seemed to cut through the oppressive hum.

But the shadows followed.

They moved like liquid smoke, coiling and twisting through the trees, faster than she thought possible. One of them darted in front of her, its glowing red eyes locking onto hers. Aria skidded to a stop, her claws extending as she bared her teeth.

"Not today," she growled, launching herself at the shadow.

A DANGEROUS ENCOUNTER

The impact was like hitting solid ice. The shadow wasn't tangible—it shifted and morphed beneath her claws, its form rippling like water. But it was strong, stronger than she'd expected. It struck back, sending her flying into a nearby tree. Pain exploded through her shoulder as she hit the bark, but she gritted her teeth and forced herself to her feet.

The alpha appeared out of nowhere, his claws glowing faintly with golden energy. He slashed through the shadow with a precision that made her wolf bristle with both respect and irritation. The creature let out a horrible screech before dissolving into nothingness.

"You're welcome," he said, not looking at her.

"I had it under control," Aria snapped, brushing dirt off her pants.

"Sure, you did." His tone was dry, but there was a flicker of amusement in his golden eyes.

She opened her mouth to argue but stopped as the hum in the air grew louder again. More shadows emerged from the trees, their red eyes glowing like embers in the dark.

"There's too many," she said, her voice low.

"For you," he said, stepping forward, his claws glowing brighter. "Stay behind me."

THE BOND AWAKENS

Aria's wolf growled in protest, hating the idea of submission. But something in the alpha's stance—steady, unyielding—gave her pause. He wasn't just fighting for dominance; he was fighting to protect her.

She clenched her fists, forcing herself to stay put as he tore through the shadows with a ferocity that left her breathless. Each strike of his claws sent ripples of energy through the air, the golden glow cutting through the darkness like a beacon.

And then she felt it.

A pull deep in her chest, like a thread connecting her to him. Her wolf stirred, not in defiance but in something that felt dangerously close to... trust.

"No," she whispered, shaking her head. But the bond wasn't something she could fight. It wasn't something she could ignore.

The alpha turned to her, his gaze sharp. "You felt that."

She glared at him. "I didn't feel anything."

His lips twitched into a faint smirk. "Liar."

Before she could respond, the last of the shadows dissolved, the clearing falling into an eerie silence. The hum faded, leaving the air still and heavy.

AFTERMATH

Aria's knees felt weak, but she refused to show it. She straightened, meeting the alpha's gaze with as much defiance as she could muster. "So, what now? You drag me back to your pack and expect me to roll over like a good little omega?"

His expression darkened, the amusement in his eyes replaced by something far more serious. "You don't get it, do you? This isn't about my pack. This is about survival."

"I've been surviving just fine on my own."

"You've been running," he said sharply. "There's a difference."

The words hit harder than she expected, and she hated that he was right. But she wouldn't let him see that. Not yet.

"Let's get one thing straight," she said, stepping closer. "I don't trust you. And I'm not part of your pack."

"Noted," he said, his tone flat. "But you're staying with me anyway."

She opened her mouth to argue, but the look in his eyes stopped her. There was no arrogance there, no dominance—just raw determination. He wasn't giving her a choice.

For now, she would play along. But she wasn't done fighting. Not by a long shot.

CHAPTER END

The alpha turned and began walking, his golden eyes scanning the shadows. Aria hesitated, her wolf pacing uneasily beneath her skin. She glanced back at the trees, half-expecting to see the red eyes reappear.

The storm wasn't just coming — it was here. And she wasn't sure she could outrun it anymore.

CHAPTER 6

The Edge of Trust

The forest seemed quieter now, the oppressive hum gone, but the stillness carried its own weight. Aria Bennett trailed behind the alpha, her body tense and her wolf pacing beneath her skin. Every instinct screamed at her to turn and run, but she knew better. For now, sticking with him was the only option.

"Where are we going?" she asked, her tone sharp. She hated the silence between them almost as much as she hated his calm, unshakable demeanor.

He didn't turn. "Somewhere safe."

"Safe isn't real," she muttered under her breath.

He glanced back, his golden eyes narrowing. "It is if you know where to look."

The words irritated her more than they should have. She didn't trust him—couldn't trust him—but he was her best chance of surviving whatever was hunting her. Still, the weight of his presence grated against her, like a collar she couldn't remove.

THE REFUGE

The alpha led her deeper into the woods, the dense trees eventually giving way to a rocky outcrop. Tucked against the base of the cliff was a small cabin, almost invisible beneath the overgrown vines and moss-covered stones. It looked abandoned, but the faint scent of shifter lingered in the air.

Aria paused at the threshold, her wolf growling softly. "You live here?"

"Sometimes," he said, pushing the door open. The hinges creaked, revealing a sparse interior—a single bed, a table, and a fireplace filled with ash. The air smelled faintly of cedar and smoke, comforting but unfamiliar.

"Cozy," she said dryly, stepping inside. Her gaze flicked around the room, cataloging exits and potential weapons. Old habits died hard.

The alpha closed the door behind her, the sound echoing through the quiet space. "It's not much, but it'll keep the shadows out."

She frowned. "And how exactly does this place do that?"

"Wards," he said simply, gesturing to faint carvings etched into the wooden beams. "Old magic. The shadows can't cross them."

Her stomach twisted at the thought of the glowing red eyes from earlier. "Convenient."

He shrugged, moving to the fireplace and kneeling to stir the ashes. "You can thank my pack's ancestors for that."

A FRAGILE PEACE

Aria dropped her pack onto the table, watching him closely. He moved with a practiced efficiency, his actions deliberate and calm. It annoyed her how unaffected he seemed by everything—like the encounter with the shadows had been nothing more than a minor inconvenience.

"Do you ever show emotion?" she asked, crossing her arms.

He glanced at her, his expression unreadable. "What would you like me to show? Panic? Fear? That won't keep you alive."

"I don't need you to keep me alive," she shot back, her voice rising.

"Clearly, you do," he said, standing and brushing ash from his hands. His golden eyes locked onto hers, and for a moment, she felt the weight of his presence like a physical force. "You've been lucky so far, Aria. But luck runs out."

The truth in his words hit harder than she wanted to admit. She looked away, her jaw tightening. "I'm not a damsel."

"No," he agreed, his tone softening. "You're a fighter. But even fighters need allies."

The words hung in the air between them, heavy and unspoken.

UNWELCOME TRUTHS

As the fire crackled to life, the alpha leaned against the table, his gaze steady on her. "You've been running for years, haven't you? Ever wonder why the shadows didn't find you before now?"

She stiffened, her wolf bristling at the question. "What are you getting at?"

"They don't just hunt at random," he said. "Something changed. Something about you."

Aria's mind raced, the memory of the bond stirring in her chest. She pushed it aside. "I didn't do anything."

He tilted his head, studying her. "Bonds don't lie, Aria."

Her heart skipped a beat, but she forced herself to glare at him. "There is no bond."

He smirked, the faintest curve of his lips infuriatingly smug. "Keep telling yourself that."

Before she could respond, a faint noise outside drew both their attention. The alpha's posture shifted instantly, his claws extending as his golden eyes narrowed.

"Stay here," he ordered.

She bristled. "I'm not—"

"Stay," he repeated, his tone leaving no room for argument. He moved to the door, opening it silently and stepping into the night.

A SILENT THREAT

The cabin felt suffocating in his absence, the walls pressing in as Aria strained to hear anything beyond the crackle of the fire. Her wolf growled softly, restless and uneasy.

Minutes passed. Then more.

She couldn't take it anymore. Grabbing her claws from her belt, she moved to the door, easing it open just enough to peer outside. The alpha stood at the edge of the clearing, his stance rigid, his claws glowing faintly with that golden energy she couldn't quite understand.

But it wasn't the alpha that made her breath catch.

Beyond him, the shadows had returned. Dozens of them, their red eyes glowing in the darkness like embers scattered across the night.

One of the shadows stepped forward, its form shifting and coiling unnaturally. It didn't attack. Instead, it spoke, its voice a low, guttural growl that seemed to vibrate through the ground.

"She belongs to us."

Aria's blood turned to ice.

CHAPTER END

The alpha didn't flinch, his claws blazing brighter as he stepped forward. "Not anymore."

The shadow hissed, its red eyes narrowing as the others began to move.

Aria's grip on the door tightened, her heart hammering in her chest. For the first time, she realized the storm wasn't just about her.

It was about them all.

CHAPTER 7

The shadows pressed forward, their red eyes glowing like embers in the dark. Aria Bennett barely breathed as she watched from the cabin's doorway, her wolf pacing restlessly beneath her skin. Every instinct screamed at her to run, but she couldn't tear her eyes away from the alpha.

He stood like a wall between her and the encroaching danger, his claws blazing with golden energy that pulsed faintly against the oppressive dark.

"She belongs to us," the shadow hissed again, its voice low and guttural, vibrating through the air like a living thing.

The alpha stepped forward, his golden eyes burning. "Not while I'm here."

The shadow paused, its form coiling and shifting unnaturally. The others behind it moved closer, a wall of darkness closing in. "You think you can protect her?" the creature snarled. "She is marked. She is ours."

Aria's stomach twisted at the words. *Marked.* Her wolf growled in protest, a low, uneasy sound that matched the dread curling in her chest. She didn't want to be anyone's possession — **not the shadows', not the alpha's.**

THE ALPHA'S POWER

The alpha didn't respond. Instead, he raised his hand, the golden glow around his claws intensifying. The air crackled with energy, a sharp, electric hum that sent shivers down Aria's spine.

The lead shadow recoiled slightly, its red eyes narrowing. "You think your light will stop us? You cannot hold back the dark forever."

"Maybe not forever," the alpha said evenly. "But long enough."

He struck without warning, his claws slashing through the air. The golden energy rippled outward, cutting through the nearest shadows like a blade through smoke. They dissolved with a shriek, their forms unraveling into nothingness.

But the others didn't flee. They surged forward instead, their movements faster, more frantic. Aria's heart pounded as the alpha met them head-on, his strikes precise and unrelenting. Each attack sent shockwaves of energy through the clearing, momentarily illuminating the night in bursts of gold.

Yet for every shadow he destroyed, more seemed to take its place.

ARIA'S CHOICE

From the doorway, Aria gripped the frame tightly, her claws digging into the wood. She couldn't just stand there. Her wolf growled, urging her to move, to fight. *You can't let him do this alone.*

"No," she whispered, shaking her head. "I don't trust him."

But trust didn't matter right now. Survival did.

Before she could second-guess herself, she grabbed her belt, slipping her own claws onto her fingers. The steel was cold and familiar, a comfort against the fear threatening to consume her. Taking a deep breath, she stepped outside.

The alpha glanced back, his golden eyes narrowing. "I told you to stay."

"And I told you I don't take orders," she snapped, her voice steady despite the fear clawing at her chest.

For a moment, he looked like he might argue, but another wave of shadows surged forward, cutting the exchange short. Aria didn't hesitate. She launched herself at the nearest one, her claws slicing through its smoky form. It let out a high-pitched shriek before dissolving, its red eyes fading into the night.

The alpha's gaze flicked to her briefly, something unreadable passing across his face. Then he turned back to the fight, his strikes growing more ferocious.

A STRANGE CONNECTION

As the battle raged, Aria became aware of something strange—a faint hum, deep in her chest. It wasn't the oppressive noise of the shadows. This was softer, warmer, like a thread of light weaving through her veins.

Each time the alpha struck, the hum grew stronger, resonating with the golden energy of his claws. And when she moved, her attacks seemed more precise, more effective, as if guided by something beyond herself.

The bond. Her wolf's voice was quiet, almost reverent.

"No," she muttered under her breath, shaking her head. But the connection was undeniable. Every time the alpha's energy surged, she felt it, too—a pulsing warmth that steadied her movements and amplified her strength.

The realization made her blood run cold. She didn't want this bond, didn't ask for it. But right now, it was the only thing keeping her alive.

A TEMPORARY VICTORY

The last of the shadows dissolved with a final shriek, leaving the clearing eerily silent. Aria stood panting, her claws slick with a strange, blackened residue that faded almost instantly. Her wolf was quiet now, watching, waiting.

The alpha straightened, his golden eyes scanning the treeline. He was breathing hard, his shoulders tense, but his stance was still steady, still unyielding. "They'll be back," he said after a moment, his voice low. "This was just a test."

"A test?" Aria's voice was sharper than she intended, her fear spilling into anger. "For what?"

"To see if you're worth the effort," he replied bluntly, his gaze locking onto hers. "And now they know you are."

Her stomach twisted at the words, but she forced herself to meet his gaze. "So what now? You drag me back to your pack and hope they don't follow?"

He shook his head, a faint smirk tugging at his lips. "You're not ready for my pack."

"Then what's your plan, Alpha?" she snapped. "Because I'm not just going to sit here and wait for them to come back."

His smirk faded, replaced by something colder, more calculating. "The plan is simple. We find out what they want. And we stop them."

Aria crossed her arms, her claws retracting. "And by 'we,' you mean me doing what you say?"

"By 'we,'" he said evenly, "I mean you learning how to survive."

<hr>

CHAPTER END

Aria glared at him, her wolf growling softly. She didn't like his tone, didn't like the way he assumed she'd just fall in line. But deep down, she knew he was right. She wasn't ready. Not yet.

The storm was still raging. And if she wanted to survive, she'd have to fight harder than she ever had before.

CHAPTER 8

Fire and Shadow

Aria Bennett sat near the dying fire in the cabin, her knees drawn tightly to her chest. An uneasy silence filled the space around her, the weight of lingering tension heavy in the air. Beneath her skin, her wolf paced restlessly, a constant reminder that the battle was far from over.

The alpha leaned against the doorway; his golden eyes fixed on the treeline. He hadn't said much since the shadows disappeared, but his presence filled the space like a storm cloud. The air between them was thick with unspoken words, their earlier argument still fresh.

"You're not going to tell me anything, are you?" Aria asked, breaking the silence. Her voice was low, edged with exhaustion but sharp enough to draw his attention.

He glanced at her; his expression unreadable. *"What do you want me to say?"*

"How about the truth? Why are they after me? What do they want?" She stood, crossing her arms. "And don't give me that 'because you're an omega' line. This feels bigger than that."

The alpha's gaze softened, but his tone remained guarded. "It is bigger. But knowing won't change the fact that you're their target."

Aria clenched her fists. "Then why don't you just leave me to deal with it? Why stick around?"

"Because if I do, you'll be dead by morning," he said bluntly. "And whether you believe it or not, keeping you alive is the only way any of us survive."

THE TRUTH BENEATH

The fire popped, sending a small spark into the air. Aria stared at it, her thoughts churning. She hated his cryptic answers, hated the way he seemed to hold all the cards. But most of all, she hated that he was right.

Her voice softened. "What are the shadows?"

The alpha hesitated, his golden eyes narrowing. "They're not alive, not in the way we understand. They're fragments of the Old Ones—pieces of their will given form. They scout, test, and claim, all in preparation for what's coming."

"And what's coming?" Aria asked, her throat tightening.

He sighed, running a hand through his dark hair. "The Old Ones aren't just stories, Aria. They're waking. And if they rise, it won't just be you or me or this pack that's at risk. It'll be everyone."

Her stomach churned, the weight of his words settling over her like a heavy blanket. "Why me?" she whispered. "Why do they care about me?"

"Because you're an omega," he said simply. "And because you're unbound. Omegas are anchors, Aria. You stabilize pack bonds, strengthen them. But unbound, you're something else entirely. You're a wild card—a source of raw power without ties. To them, you're the perfect conduit."

Her pulse quickened. *"A conduit for what?"*

"For them," he said, his voice grim. "To tether themselves to this world."

<hr />

AN UNEASY ALLIANCE

Aria sank back onto the log, her claws twitching at her sides. The pieces were falling into place, but the picture they formed was terrifying. She was more than a target — she was a tool. And if the Old Ones succeeded in claiming her…

She shook her head, forcing the thought away. "So what's the plan? You said we had to stop them. How?"

The alpha stepped closer, his presence as steadying as it was unsettling. "First, we train."

Aria raised an eyebrow. "Train? You think I'm just going to let you boss me around?"

"You don't have a choice," he said evenly. "You need to learn how to fight them. And I need to figure out why the bond is so strong."

The mention of the bond sent a jolt through her, the memory of that hum in her chest flashing in her mind. She glared at him. "The bond is nothing."

He smirked, the faintest hint of amusement breaking through his stoic exterior. "Keep telling yourself that, little rogue. But it's the only reason you're alive."

She bristled, her wolf growling softly. "I didn't ask for it."

"No," he said, his tone softening. "But you can't run from it."

THE CALL OF THE SHADOWS

Before she could respond, a distant sound cut through the night—a low, resonant hum that made her blood run cold. The alpha stiffened, his golden eyes snapping toward the treeline.

"They're coming," he said, his voice sharp. "Get inside. Now."

Aria hesitated, her claws extending as her wolf rose to the surface. "I'm not hiding."

"Aria," he said, his tone dangerous. "This isn't a fight we can win. Not yet."

The urgency in his voice sent a shiver through her. Reluctantly, she stepped back toward the cabin, her eyes never leaving the darkened woods. The hum grew louder, vibrating through the air like an unspoken warning.

As the alpha moved to follow, he paused, his gaze locking onto hers. "When this is over, you'll listen to me. No more running. No more arguing. Do you understand?"

She opened her mouth to argue but stopped herself. For once, her wolf agreed with him.

"Fine," she said quietly, her voice barely audible over the hum. "But this doesn't mean I trust you."

He nodded once before stepping outside, the door closing behind him with a resolute thud.

CHAPTER END HOOK

Aria stood in the cabin's shadowed interior, her breath shallow as she stared at the closed door. The hum grew louder, closer, until it felt like it was inside her chest. Her wolf growled, a low, uneasy sound that sent shivers down her spine.

And then the first red eyes appeared in the dark.

CHAPTER 9

Beneath the Surface

The first pair of red eyes glared through the darkness, followed by another, and another. Aria Bennett's breath hitched as the shadows seemed to multiply, their forms coiling and twisting unnaturally at the edge of the cabin's wards.

The low hum in the air grew stronger, vibrating through the floorboards beneath her feet. Her wolf bristled, its growl echoing faintly in her mind. *Danger.*

Through the small window, she saw the alpha standing firm, his claws glowing faintly with that golden energy. He didn't move, didn't flinch, even as the shadows pressed closer.

What is he waiting for? Aria thought, her hands twitching at her sides. Every instinct screamed at her to run, to fight, to do anything but stand idle. Yet she stayed rooted, her chest tight with the weight of her own helplessness.

A TEST OF TRUST

The hum became a low roar, the sound pressing against her ears like a physical force. The shadows moved closer, their red eyes glowing brighter, and then—silence. The sound cut off so abruptly it left her head spinning, the sudden quiet almost worse than the noise.

The lead shadow, its form taller and more defined than the others, stepped forward. It didn't speak this time. Instead, it raised an arm—long and skeletal, like smoke solidified— and slammed it against the invisible barrier of the wards.

The cabin trembled, the impact reverberating through the walls. Aria stumbled back, her claws extending instinctively. She heard a low snarl outside and realized it was the alpha.

The shadow hit the barrier again, and again, each strike louder, harder. Cracks of light formed along the edges of the wards, flickering like lightning.

"They're breaking through," Aria whispered, her voice trembling. She turned toward the door, her heart pounding. "He's not going to be able to stop them."

A LEAP OF FAITH

Without thinking, she moved. Her claws scraped against the doorframe as she flung it open, stepping into the clearing. The cold night air hit her like a slap, but she ignored it, her focus locked on the alpha.

He turned sharply, his golden eyes blazing. "What are you doing?"

"Helping," she said, her voice steady despite the chaos around her.

His jaw tightened. **"Get back inside."**

"No." She stepped forward, her wolf growling low in agreement. "You said it yourself—I need to learn. So let me."

For a moment, she thought he might argue. But then his gaze softened, just slightly, and he gave a single nod. "Stay close."

THE SHADOWS' FURY

The lead shadow screeched, its sound cutting through the air like jagged glass. It slammed against the wards again, and this time, the barrier shattered with a sound like breaking ice. The golden glow of the wards faded, leaving only darkness.

"Now," the alpha said sharply, his claws igniting with golden light.

The shadows surged forward, their forms twisting and writhing as they lunged toward them. Aria barely had time to react before the first one reached her, its red eyes locking onto hers. She slashed with her claws, the steel cutting through its smoky form. It shrieked and dissipated, but two more took its place.

Her movements were instinctual, her wolf lending her speed and precision. Yet for every shadow she struck down, the energy it took left her more drained.

"Focus!" the alpha's voice cut through the chaos, steady and commanding. "Stay grounded!"

She snarled, her wolf pushing her forward as another shadow lunged. This time, she felt it — the hum in her chest, the connection to the alpha's energy. Her claws glowed faintly, and when she struck, the shadow dissolved instantly, its shriek cutting short.

The alpha glanced at her, surprise flickering in his eyes before he turned back to the fight. "Good. Keep going."

A NEW ENEMY

The tide began to turn. Together, they cut through the shadows, their movements almost synchronized. Aria hated how natural it felt, how the bond seemed to guide her actions, but she couldn't deny its effectiveness.

And then the air changed.

The shadows pulled back suddenly, their forms retreating to the edges of the clearing. The lead shadow didn't follow. Instead, it shifted, growing taller, its red eyes blazing brighter. When it spoke, its voice was layered, like many voices speaking in unison.

"You cannot win."

The alpha stepped forward, his golden claws glowing brighter. "Watch me."

The shadow didn't flinch. Instead, it raised both arms, its form expanding, coiling outward like smoke spreading through the air. The temperature dropped, frost forming on the grass beneath their feet.

Aria's breath clouded in the freezing air, her claws trembling as she readied herself. "What is it doing?"

The alpha didn't answer. He moved in front of her, his stance protective. "Stay behind me."

"No," she said, her voice firm. **"We do this together."**

He glanced back at her, something flickering in his expression—pride, maybe, or respect. He nodded once. "Together."

CHAPTER END

The shadow surged forward, its form splitting into dozens of tendrils, each one writhing with dark energy. Aria braced herself, her claws glowing faintly with that golden light.

The bond pulsed between them, stronger than ever, as the shadow's attack crashed down like a tidal wave.

CHAPTER 10

The Tide Turns

The wave of shadow energy crashed toward them, fast and unrelenting. Aria Bennett braced herself, her claws glowing faintly with the golden energy that now pulsed in time with the alpha's. Her wolf snarled, urging her to strike, but the sheer force of the attack froze her in place.

The alpha moved first.

With a roar, his claws slashed through the tendrils, the golden light blazing brighter than before. The shadow recoiled, its form splintering but not dissipating. The lead tendril re-formed quickly, snapping back like a whip aimed directly at him.

"Move!" Aria shouted, lunging forward. Her claws caught the tendril mid-strike, the golden energy in her grip flaring as the shadow recoiled with a screech.

The alpha turned to her, his golden eyes narrowing. "I told you to stay behind me."

"And I told you I don't take orders," she shot back, her voice tight with adrenaline. She didn't wait for his response. The bond pulsed stronger now, guiding her movements as she struck again and again, her claws finding their mark with unerring precision.

THE SHADOW'S EVOLUTION

The shadow hissed, its form coiling tighter, more defined. It wasn't retreating. It was adapting.

The red eyes shifted, locking onto Aria now. The temperature dropped further, frost spreading across the ground beneath her feet. Her breath came in shallow bursts, visible in the icy air.

"Stay with me," the alpha said sharply, stepping closer. His voice cut through her mounting fear, grounding her.

The shadow surged forward, its tendrils multiplying and splitting. Aria and the alpha moved as one, their strikes synchronized, but for every tendril they destroyed, more appeared.

"This isn't working," Aria panted, her movements slowing under the shadow's relentless assault. "It's too strong."

"It's not strength," the alpha said, his golden eyes scanning the shadow's form. "It's persistence. We need to disrupt it."

"How?" she asked, slashing at another tendril.

"Together," he said simply.

A LEAP OF FAITH

The bond between them pulsed again, stronger this time. Aria felt it deep in her chest, a steady hum that resonated with the alpha's energy. She hated the way it felt—comforting, steady—but she couldn't deny its power.

"What do I do?" she asked reluctantly.

"Follow my lead," he said, his tone steady but urgent. "Focus on the bond. Let it guide you."

Aria gritted her teeth, pushing past her resistance. She closed her eyes for a brief moment, tuning into the hum of the bond. It was warm, steady, and terrifyingly intimate, but it brought clarity. When she opened her eyes, the shadow's form seemed sharper, its movements more predictable.

The alpha struck first, his claws blazing as he drove the shadow back. Aria followed, her strikes precise and deliberate. The golden energy between them flared brighter, and for the first time, the shadow faltered.

"It's working," she said, her voice filled with cautious hope.

"Don't stop," the alpha growled, his strikes growing more powerful. "We finish this now."

THE FINAL BLOW

The shadow screeched, its form unraveling as the golden energy tore through it. Its red eyes dimmed, flickering like dying embers. Aria felt the bond pulse one last time, stronger than ever, as she and the alpha moved in unison.

With a final, blinding strike, the shadow collapsed, its form dissipating into a cloud of black smoke. The clearing fell silent, the oppressive hum vanishing as quickly as it had come.

Aria stumbled back, her claws retracting as exhaustion hit her like a wave. Her wolf was quiet now, watching, waiting.

The alpha stood motionless for a moment, his golden eyes scanning the clearing. When he turned to her, his expression was unreadable.

"You did well," he said finally, his voice low.

Aria bristled, her exhaustion making her temper flare. "Don't patronize me."

"I'm not," he said simply. "You're stronger than I expected."

She stared at him, unsure how to respond. The bond still hummed faintly in her chest, a reminder of their connection. She hated it, but she couldn't deny its power.

THE AFTERMATH

The frost on the ground began to melt, the air warming as the shadow's presence faded completely. Aria moved to the edge of the clearing; her steps unsteady. She needed space, needed to think.

"Aria." The alpha's voice stopped her. She turned, meeting his gaze.

"They'll be back," he said, his tone serious. "And next time, they won't send scouts."

Her stomach tightened at his words. "So what do we do?"

"We get stronger," he said simply. "And we prepare."

"For what?" she asked, her voice barely above a whisper.

His golden eyes burned with a quiet intensity. "For war."

CHAPTER END HOOK

The word hung in the air, heavy and final. Aria turned away, her jaw tightening. The storm was far from over. And this time, there would be no running.

Chapter 11

Forging Fire

The morning light filtered through the trees, casting long shadows over the clearing. Aria Bennett stood at its edge, her claws extended as she faced off against the alpha. Her chest rose and fell with controlled breaths, her wolf bristling beneath her skin. She hated this—being watched, judged—but she couldn't deny the tension in the air made her sharper.

"You're holding back," the alpha said, his golden eyes fixed on her. His tone was calm, almost bored, which irritated her more than she cared to admit.

"I'm pacing myself," Aria shot back, her claws twitching.

"Pacing yourself won't keep you alive," he countered. "Again."

She growled low in her throat, forcing herself to step forward. The bond hummed faintly between them, guiding her movements, but she pushed it away. She didn't want to rely on him, on this... connection. She wanted to win on her own terms.

She struck, her claws slicing through the air with precision. The alpha dodged easily, his movements fluid and deliberate. Before she could recover, he was behind her, his claws stopping an inch from her neck.

"You're predictable," he said, his voice low. "You fight like you're scared."

"I'm not scared," Aria snapped, spinning to face him.

"Then prove it," he said, stepping back to give her space. "Because the shadows won't wait for you to figure out what you want."

FRUSTRATION AND RESOLVE

Aria's claws retracted as she let out a frustrated breath. Her wolf growled softly, mirroring her irritation. "What's the point of this?" she asked, her voice sharper than she intended. "You can handle the shadows. You don't need me."

The alpha crossed his arms, his golden eyes narrowing. "You're not just fighting for yourself anymore. You're fighting for everyone. The sooner you understand that, the better."

His words settled over her like a heavy weight. She hated how they made sense, how they pressed against the walls she'd built around herself. She looked away, her jaw tightening. "I didn't ask for this."

"Neither did I," he said, his tone softening. "But here we are."

She didn't respond, her mind racing. The bond pulsed faintly in her chest, a constant reminder of their connection. She hated it—hated him—but deep down, she knew he was right. If she wanted to survive, if she wanted to win, she had to stop fighting alone.

"Fine," she said finally, meeting his gaze. "What's next?"

THE TEST

The alpha tilted his head slightly, as if surprised by her sudden resolve. "We take this further."

"What does that mean?" she asked, narrowing her eyes.

He didn't answer. Instead, he stepped back, gesturing toward the woods. "Follow me."

Aria hesitated, her wolf growling softly in protest, but she forced herself to move. The forest was quiet as they walked, the only sounds the crunch of leaves beneath their feet and the faint rustle of the wind.

After a few minutes, they reached a clearing. In its center stood a stone circle, its surface etched with runes that pulsed faintly with golden light. Aria frowned, her claws twitching instinctively. "What is this?"

"A training ground," the alpha said, stepping into the circle. "It was built by my pack centuries ago, back when the Old Ones were just myths. The runes amplify energy, make it easier to push limits. But they also test you."

Aria crossed her arms, her wolf uneasy. "Test me how?"

"You'll see," he said, his tone cryptic. "Step inside."

She glared at him, her instincts screaming at her to stay away. But curiosity and stubbornness pushed her forward. She stepped into the circle, the air shifting around her immediately. The bond pulsed stronger now, resonating with the runes beneath her feet.

FACING HERSELF

The clearing faded, replaced by darkness. Aria's heart pounded as she looked around, her claws extending instinctively. "What is this?" she called out, her voice echoing.

No answer came. Instead, a figure emerged from the shadows — familiar, yet wrong. It was her, but not her. This version of herself had glowing red eyes, its claws dripping with blackened energy. It tilted its head, a twisted smile curling its lips.

"You think you're strong?" the shadow-Aria hissed, its voice layered with malice. "You're nothing but prey. Always running, always hiding."

Aria's wolf snarled, its energy surging as she took a defensive stance. "You're not real."

The shadow laughed, the sound cold and sharp. "I'm every fear you've ever had. Every weakness you refuse to admit. And I'm stronger than you."

It lunged, fast and vicious, and Aria barely dodged in time. The fight was chaotic, every strike forcing her to confront her own insecurities. The shadow's words echoed in her mind, taunting her, tearing at her defenses.

But the bond pulsed again, stronger this time. It steadied her, grounded her. She felt the alpha's presence faintly, like a distant warmth, and it gave her strength.

"You're wrong," Aria said, her voice firm. She struck with all her might, her claws glowing faintly with golden light. The shadow shrieked, its form dissolving into smoke.

When the darkness cleared, the alpha was standing at the edge of the circle, his golden eyes watching her intently.

THE AFTERMATH

Aria stepped out of the circle, her body trembling with exhaustion. She met the alpha's gaze, her voice unsteady. "What was that?"

"A reflection," he said simply. "The runes force you to face your greatest weaknesses."

She swallowed hard, her claws retracting. "And if I'd lost?"

"You didn't," he said, his tone softer now. "That's what matters."

Aria looked away, the bond pulsing faintly in her chest. She still didn't trust him, but for the first time, she felt a sliver of understanding. If they were going to win this war, she needed him. And he needed her.

<hr>

CHAPTER END

As they walked back to the cabin, the alpha spoke, his voice quiet. "Tomorrow, we go deeper. There's more to you than you realize, Aria. It's time you saw it for yourself."

The bond pulsed again, stronger than before. And for the first time, Aria didn't push it away.

CHAPTER 12

Echoes of Power

The next morning came with the kind of heavy stillness that made the air feel thick. Ari stood outside the cabin; her arms crossed as the alpha prepared the training circle once more. Her wolf growled faintly, restless and uneasy.

*"**I'm not going back in there,**" she said flatly, her claws tapping against her arms. "Whatever those runes are, they're worse than the shadows."

The alpha didn't look up, his golden eyes scanning the runes as they began to glow faintly. "You survived, didn't you?"

"Barely." Her voice was sharp, but her chest tightened at the memory of facing her shadow-self. "What's the point of this anyway? It's not like those things are going to show up and taunt me to death."

The alpha finally turned; his gaze steady. "You think the shadows are your biggest threat?" He took a step closer, his voice dropping. "You're not fighting them, Aria. You're fighting yourself. If you can't control that, you're already dead."

The words hit harder than she expected, but she refused to let him see it. She squared her shoulders, meeting his gaze head-on. "I'm not afraid of myself."

"Then prove it," he said simply.

A NEW CHALLENGE

The bond pulsed faintly as Aria stepped into the circle again, the air shifting around her. This time, the runes' glow felt warmer, steadier, but it did little to ease her tension. The alpha stood at the edge, watching her with that infuriating calm.

"What now?" she asked, her voice laced with irritation. "Another round with my evil twin?"

"Not exactly," he said, crossing his arms. "This time, you're not alone."

The air shifted, and the bond pulsed stronger. Aria turned sharply as a figure materialized beside her—it was the alpha. Or at least, a version of him. This version radiated pure dominance, his golden eyes blazing with power.

"What is this?" Aria demanded, her claws extending instinctively.

"A reflection of me," the real alpha said from the edge of the circle. "The runes amplify energy. You'll face the worst of what you think I am."

"Great," she muttered, her wolf growling low. "Just what I needed—two of you."

The reflection struck first, moving faster than Aria anticipated. She barely dodged the glowing claws, her wolf snapping to the surface. The fight was chaotic, every strike forcing her to anticipate, adapt, and counter.

"You're holding back," the real alpha called out, his voice cutting through the chaos. "Stop thinking. Trust the bond."

"I don't trust the bond!" Aria shouted, dodging another strike. Her claws slashed through the reflection's arm, but it barely slowed. "And I don't trust you."

The reflection lunged again, its claws glowing brighter. Aria's wolf roared in defiance, and for a moment, the bond pulsed so strongly it felt like fire in her veins. She moved instinctively, her claws glowing faintly as they met the reflection's strike head-on.

The resulting clash sent a shockwave through the circle, the golden energy flaring brightly. When the light faded, the reflection was gone, and Aria stood alone, panting heavily.

THE ALPHA'S APPROVAL

She stumbled out of the circle, her legs trembling. The alpha caught her arm before she fell, his grip steady but firm.

"Better," he said simply.

Aria jerked her arm away, glaring at him. "What the hell was that?"

"A lesson," he said, his tone calm. "You rely too much on anger. It makes you predictable."

She clenched her fists, her claws retracting. "I handled it, didn't I?"

"Barely," he countered. "You keep fighting the bond, fighting yourself. That's what they'll exploit."

"They?" Aria asked, narrowing her eyes.

"The Old Ones," he said, his golden eyes serious. "The shadows aren't their only weapons. They'll use your fears, your doubts, and your anger against you. If you don't control them, they'll control you."

Her stomach twisted at his words, but she refused to let him see her falter. "I don't need a lecture."

"No," he said softly. "You need the truth."

A GLIMPSE OF THE SHIFTER WORLD

That evening, as the sun dipped below the horizon, the alpha led her to a ridge overlooking the valley below. The sight was breathtaking—rolling hills dotted with patches of forest, the distant glow of what looked like a town nestled against a river.

"What is this place?" Aria asked, her voice quieter now.

"Neutral territory," the alpha said. "Beyond that ridge is the edge of pack lands."

She stiffened, her wolf growling softly. "We're close to your pack?"

"Yes," he said, his tone steady. "And others."

The tension in her chest grew. She'd avoided packs for so long, the thought of being near one again sent her instincts into overdrive. "Why are we here?"

"Because this fight isn't just about you," he said, his gaze scanning the horizon. "If we're going to stop the Old Ones, we'll need allies. Packs, rogues, anyone willing to stand."

She frowned, crossing her arms. "You think they'll listen to you?"

"They'll listen to you," he said, his golden eyes locking onto hers. "An unbound omega is more than a threat. You're a symbol. And whether you like it or not, they'll follow you."

Her heart raced at his words, the weight of them settling over her. "I didn't ask for this."

"No," he said softly. "But it's yours anyway."

CHAPTER END

As the first stars appeared in the night sky, Aria turned back toward the valley. The town's lights flickered like distant fireflies, a beacon in the growing dark.

The bond pulsed faintly, a reminder of the fight ahead. For the first time, Aria didn't push it away.

"Then let's make them listen," she said, her voice steady.

CHAPTER 13

The Weight of Leadership

The cool night air lingered as Aria Bennett stood on the ridge, her gaze locked on the glowing town below. The alpha stood beside her, his golden eyes scanning the horizon. His presence was steady, unwavering, but the bond between them hummed with something heavier tonight—expectation.

"Tell me about them," Aria said finally, breaking the silence. Her voice was low, as though speaking too loudly would shatter her resolve. "The packs. What am I walking into?"

The alpha's expression didn't change, but his gaze softened slightly. "The packs are strong, but fractured. Each one guards its own interests, its own borders. They'll fight for survival, but unity doesn't come easily."

She frowned, her claws twitching at her sides. "And you think they'll unite for me? For some rogue omega they've never even heard of?"

"They'll have to," he said simply. "Because the Old Ones won't stop with you. If they rise, there will be no borders left to guard."

His words settled heavily over her, and Aria turned her gaze back to the town. "They'll want something in return," she said quietly. "They always do."

The alpha's jaw tightened. "They'll want to test you. To see if you're worth following."

"And if I'm not?" she asked, her voice sharper now.

"They won't follow," he said bluntly. "**But you are.**"

CROSSING THE LINE

The journey into neutral territory was quieter than Aria expected. The forest grew thinner as they descended from the ridge, the trees replaced by rolling hills and narrow dirt paths. The tension in her chest grew with every step, her wolf restless beneath her skin.

"They'll smell me coming," she said after a while, her claws tapping against her belt. "What's the plan when they decide I'm a threat?"

"They won't attack," the alpha said confidently.

She snorted. "You sound sure."

"I am," he said, glancing back at her. "Because I'll be with you."

Her wolf growled softly, a mix of irritation and something she refused to name. She didn't like the idea of relying on him, but she couldn't deny the truth in his words. His presence was a shield, whether she wanted it or not.

THE FIRST ENCOUNTER

The town wasn't what Aria expected. It wasn't sprawling or loud. It was quiet, almost serene, its streets lined with modest buildings and shifter symbols carved into the wooden posts. A faint scent lingered in the air — one that made her wolf bristle. Pack territory.

They stopped at the edge of the main street, and the alpha motioned for her to wait. "Let me speak first."

"Fine," Aria said, crossing her arms. "But I'm not hiding."

He smirked faintly, something almost like approval flickering in his golden eyes. "I didn't think you would."

A figure approached from one of the buildings — a tall man with dark eyes and a broad frame. His scent was sharp, commanding, but it lacked the overwhelming dominance of the alpha beside her. He stopped a few feet away, his gaze flicking between them.

"Hunter," the man said, his tone cautious. "I didn't expect to see you here."

Aria froze at the name. Hunter. She rolled it over in her mind, fitting it to the alpha beside her. It felt... strange, but right.

"Warrick," the alpha — Hunter — replied evenly. "We need to talk."

Warrick's eyes narrowed slightly, his gaze settling on Aria. "And who's this?"

"An ally," Hunter said, his tone leaving no room for argument.

Warrick's lips pressed into a thin line, but he didn't challenge it. Instead, he stepped aside, motioning toward the town center. "Come in. But don't expect a warm welcome."

TENSION RISING

The town's center was a simple open space surrounded by more buildings, each marked with shifter runes. Aria felt the weight of every gaze on her as they walked — eyes filled with curiosity, suspicion, and something darker. Her wolf growled low in her chest, but she kept her head high, refusing to shrink under their scrutiny.

"They don't trust me," she said quietly, glancing at Hunter.

"They don't need to," he replied. "They just need to listen."

Warrick led them into a small hall, its walls lined with crude wooden benches. A few shifters were already waiting inside, their postures tense. As Hunter stepped forward, they straightened, their eyes fixed on him.

"We don't have time for pleasantries," Hunter said, his voice carrying through the room. "The Old Ones are moving, and they've marked an omega. If they rise, they'll come for all of us."

The room erupted in murmurs, the tension rising palpably. One of the shifters — a wiry woman with sharp features —

stood, her claws twitching. "And you expect us to believe that? You show up with some rogue and expect us to follow?"

"She's not just a rogue," Hunter said, his golden eyes locking onto hers. "She's unbound."

The murmurs stopped instantly, the weight of his words settling over the room like a storm cloud.

ARIA'S RESOLVE

Aria felt the weight of their stares, her wolf bristling under the scrutiny. She wanted to step back, to let Hunter handle this, but the bond pulsed faintly in her chest—a reminder of the fight ahead.

Taking a deep breath, she stepped forward, her voice steady. "I didn't ask for this," she said, meeting the wiry woman's gaze. "But it's happening. And if you think you can survive this on your own, you're wrong."

The room was silent for a moment, the tension thick. Then Warrick spoke, his tone measured. "If she's unbound, she's a target. That much is clear. But what makes her worth following?"

Hunter glanced at Aria; his expression unreadable. "She'll show you."

CHAPTER END

The promise hung heavy in the air as every gaze turned to Aria. The bond pulsed stronger now, a steady hum in her chest. She didn't know how she'd prove herself, but one thing was certain:

The storm was just beginning.

CHAPTER 14

The Trial

The tension in the room was thick enough to choke on. Aria Bennett felt the weight of every gaze on her, their suspicion and curiosity pressing down like a heavy fog. Her wolf growled low in her chest, restless beneath her skin. She hated this—the scrutiny, the judgment—but she refused to back down.

Hunter, standing tall beside her, spoke evenly. "The Old Ones are hunting her because she's unbound. That alone makes her a threat to them. But to us, it makes her an opportunity."

"An opportunity for what?" Warrick asked, his tone skeptical. The dark-eyed shifter leaned back against the wall, his claws tapping idly on his belt. "To die faster?"

"To fight," Hunter said sharply. "If the Old Ones rise, they'll come for all of us. We'll need every advantage we can get, and unbound omegas are rare for a reason."

Murmurs rippled through the room again, but Aria caught the undertone — fear. Not of her, but of what was coming. The weight of it made her stomach twist, but she forced herself to stand tall.

"Talk is cheap," the wiry woman from earlier said, stepping forward. Her sharp eyes locked onto Aria with a challenge that made her wolf bristle. "You want us to believe in her? She'll have to prove she's worth the risk."

THE CHALLENGE

The room fell silent at the woman's words. Hunter's golden eyes narrowed, and he stepped forward, his claws glowing faintly. "This isn't the time for petty tests, Mara. The Old Ones—"

"The Old Ones aren't here," Mara interrupted, her voice cutting through his. "She is. And if she can't hold her own, we shouldn't waste resources protecting her."

Aria's wolf snarled, and she stepped forward before she could stop herself. "I don't need your protection," she said, her voice cold. "And I don't need your approval."

Mara's lips twitched into a faint smirk. "Good. Then you won't mind a little trial."

"Mara—" Hunter's voice was a warning, but Aria cut him off.

"Fine," she said, her claws extending instinctively. "What's the trial?"

Mara raised an eyebrow, clearly surprised by her willingness. "We fight. If you can hold your own, I'll listen. If not..." She trailed off, her meaning clear.

Aria's heart pounded, but she didn't let it show. Instead, she glanced at Hunter, her voice steady. "I don't need you to speak for me."

Hunter's jaw tightened, but he stepped back, his golden eyes locking onto hers. "Don't hold back."

THE FIGHT

The trial was set in the open square, the crowd of shifters forming a wide circle around them. The murmurs had grown louder now, buzzing with anticipation. Aria felt their eyes on her, felt the weight of their doubts and curiosity. Her wolf growled low, eager for the fight.

Mara stood across from her, claws glinting faintly in the moonlight. Her stance was relaxed, confident, but there was a sharpness to her movements that put Aria on edge.

"You ready, rogue?" Mara called; her tone almost playful.

Aria didn't answer. She let her claws extend fully, her wolf rising to the surface. The bond pulsed faintly in her chest, but she shoved it aside. This was her fight.

Mara struck first, moving faster than Aria anticipated. Her claws slashed through the air, forcing Aria to dodge quickly. The crowd murmured, their voices a distant hum as Aria countered with a swipe of her own. Her claws grazed Mara's arm, but the older shifter barely flinched.

"You'll have to do better than that," Mara said, her voice taunting.

Aria snarled, her wolf snapping at her skin. She moved faster this time, her claws striking with precision. Mara blocked her easily, but the bond pulsed again, stronger now. Aria felt it guiding her movements, sharpening her instincts.

Her next strike hit its mark, her claws slicing through Mara's shoulder. The older shifter hissed, her eyes flashing with irritation, but she didn't back down. Instead, she pressed harder, her strikes coming faster, more aggressive.

THE TURNING POINT

The fight became a blur of movement, each strike and dodge pushing Aria closer to her limits. Her breath came in sharp bursts, her muscles burning, but she refused to falter. The bond pulsed steadily now, a hum of energy that steadied her when her strength wavered.

Mara lunged again, her claws aiming for Aria's side. This time, Aria moved instinctively, her claws glowing faintly with golden light. She met Mara's strike head-on, the impact sending a shockwave through the square.

The crowd fell silent as Mara stumbled back, her claws retracting. She looked down at her hands, then back at Aria, her expression unreadable.

Aria straightened, her claws still glowing faintly. Her wolf was quiet now, watching, waiting.

Mara smirked, blood dripping from her shoulder. "Not bad, rogue. Not bad at all."

THE VERDICT

Hunter stepped forward, his golden eyes scanning the crowd. "You've seen what she's capable of. She's more than a rogue. She's a fighter."

The murmurs rose again, this time less hostile. Warrick stepped into the circle, his dark eyes thoughtful. "She's strong," he said, his tone measured. "But strength isn't enough."

"It's a start," Hunter said sharply. "And it's more than most of you could manage."

Aria's claws retracted as she turned to face the crowd. Her voice was steady, louder than she expected. "You don't have to trust me," she said. "But if we don't stand together, none of us will survive this."

The crowd fell silent again, her words hanging in the air. For the first time, she saw something shift in their eyes — not trust, not yet, but something close to it.

CHAPTER END HOOK

As the crowd began to disperse, Mara approached Aria, her expression unreadable. "You've got fire, rogue," she said quietly. "But fire burns out if you're not careful."

"I'll keep that in mind," Aria replied, her voice firm.

Mara smirked faintly before turning and disappearing into the crowd. Hunter stepped up beside Aria, his golden eyes warm with approval.

"You did well," he said.

"It's not over," Aria replied, her gaze fixed on the retreating shifters. The bond pulsed faintly, steady and strong. "Not even close."

CHAPTER 15

Building Alliances

The tension in the air lingered long after the fight ended. Aria Bennett felt it in the way the shifters' eyes followed her as she walked, their gazes cautious but no longer openly hostile. Her wolf was restless, prowling just beneath her skin, but she kept her head high. She had won their attention, if not their trust.

Hunter strode beside her, his golden eyes scanning the town. "You handled yourself well."

"Don't sound so surprised," Aria muttered, her voice low. Her claws tapped idly against her belt as they approached the small hall where Warrick and the other leaders waited.

"I'm not," Hunter said evenly. "But this was only the first step."

She glanced at him, irritation flaring. "Do you ever say anything encouraging?"

His lips twitched into the faintest smirk. "You don't strike me as someone who needs encouragement."

INSIDE THE HALL

The hall felt different this time — less tense, though no less serious. Warrick stood at the head of the room, his arms crossed as he watched Aria and Hunter enter. Mara leaned against the wall nearby, her sharp eyes gleaming with something that looked like approval.

"You've made your point," Warrick said, his voice steady. "She's strong. But strength alone won't unite the packs."

"I'm not asking for unity," Hunter replied, his tone calm but firm. "I'm asking for survival. And whether you like it or not, she's our best chance."

Aria's wolf growled softly, but she forced it down. She didn't need Hunter speaking for her. "If you have a better idea," she said, stepping forward, "I'm listening."

Warrick's dark eyes met hers, his expression unreadable. "It's not about ideas. It's about trust. The packs don't follow strangers, especially not rogues."

Aria clenched her fists, her claws twitching. "I'm not asking them to follow me. I'm asking them to fight."

"And they won't fight unless they believe in the cause," Mara added, her tone cutting. "Or in you."

A PLAN FORMS

Hunter stepped forward; his golden eyes sharp. "Then give us the chance to prove it. Send messengers to the other packs. Call them here."

Warrick frowned. "And if they refuse?"

"They won't," Hunter said. "Not when they hear what's at stake."

Mara straightened, her claws tapping against her side. "You're asking us to put everything on the line for a rogue and a myth. That's a hard sell, even for you."

"It's not a myth," Hunter said, his voice colder now. "The Old Ones are real, and they're moving. If we wait until they're at our doors, it'll be too late."

The room fell silent, the weight of his words settling over them like a storm cloud. Warrick exchanged a glance with Mara, then sighed. "Fine. I'll send the messengers. But don't expect miracles."

TRAINING BEGINS

The following days were a blur of preparation. The town square became a makeshift training ground, shifters gathering to hone their skills under Hunter's watchful eye. Aria threw herself into the work, her claws slicing through the air as she practiced against Mara and the others.

"You're improving," Mara said one afternoon, her voice grudgingly respectful. "Still sloppy, but better."

"Thanks," Aria said dryly, brushing dirt from her pants. Her muscles ached, her wolf restless from the constant exertion, but she refused to stop. She had something to prove—to Mara, to Hunter, to herself.

Hunter observed from a distance, his golden eyes unreadable. Aria could feel the bond humming faintly, a steady reminder of his presence. She hated how it steadied her, how it felt like a lifeline she didn't want but couldn't deny.

A NEW ALLY

On the third evening, as the sun dipped below the horizon, the first messenger arrived. It was a young woman, her lean frame tense as she approached the town square. Warrick greeted her with a nod, his expression grim.

"They're coming," the messenger said, her voice breathless. "Three packs. But they're not happy about it."

"Are they ever?" Mara muttered, earning a faint smirk from Warrick.

Aria watched from the edge of the square, her stomach twisting. The idea of facing so many pack alphas made her wolf growl uneasily. She glanced at Hunter, who stood beside her, his posture steady.

"You think they'll listen?" she asked quietly.

"They'll listen," he said. "The question is whether they'll act."

THE ARRIVAL

The next morning, the packs began to arrive. Aria stood with Hunter and the others at the edge of the square, her claws twitching nervously at her sides. The first pack strode in with confident ease, their alpha—a tall, broad-shouldered man—leading the way. His dark eyes swept over the town before landing on Aria.

"So, this is the rogue," he said, his voice dripping with skepticism. "You've been busy, Hunter."

"She's not just a rogue," Hunter said evenly. "She's unbound."

The alpha's eyebrows lifted, but his expression didn't soften. "Unbound or not, she'll have to prove herself."

Aria clenched her fists, her wolf growling softly. "I'm not here to prove anything to you."

"Then you're wasting your time," the alpha said coldly. "Because that's the only way this works."

CHAPTER END

Hunter stepped forward, his golden eyes blazing. "She's already proven herself. But if you need more, stick around."

The alpha smirked faintly, his gaze flicking back to Aria. "I will."

The bond pulsed faintly in Aria's chest as she met his gaze, her voice steady. "Good. I'm just getting started."

CHAPTER 16

The Test of Trust

The packs filled the town square, their presence heavy with tension. Aria Bennett stood near the edge, her posture rigid as she watched the alphas gather. Their scents mixed in the air—sharp, earthy, and charged with dominance. Her wolf paced beneath her skin, uneasy but alert.

Hunter stood at her side, his golden eyes scanning the crowd. His presence was steady, grounding, but the bond between them hummed faintly, a reminder of the growing weight on her shoulders.

"They're watching you," he said quietly, his tone even.

"I noticed," Aria muttered, her claws twitching at her sides. "What happens if they decide I'm not worth it?"

"They won't," Hunter replied. "Because you won't give them a choice."

AN UNEXPECTED CHALLENGE

The alpha of the first pack, the broad-shouldered man who had spoken the day before, stepped forward. His dark eyes swept over Aria, sharp and calculating. "You talk big for a rogue," he said, his tone laced with skepticism. "But words won't hold the line when the Old Ones come."

Aria's jaw tightened, her wolf bristling at his tone. "What do you suggest, then? Another trial?"

"Not just a trial," he said, a faint smirk curling his lips. "A hunt."

The murmurs in the crowd grew louder, the tension thickening. Hunter's golden eyes narrowed, his claws twitching at his sides. "This isn't the time for games, Carrick."

"It's not a game," Carrick said, his gaze locked on Aria. "If she's as strong as you say, let her prove it. There's a rogue shadow reported near the southern woods. If she can take it down, we'll talk about an alliance."

Aria glanced at Hunter, her heart pounding. She hated the idea of being paraded around like a trophy, but she also knew this was her chance to show them what she could do.

"I'll do it," she said before Hunter could argue.

The murmurs stopped instantly, the crowd turning to her with a mix of surprise and curiosity. Carrick raised an eyebrow, his smirk widening. "Bold. Let's see if you can back it up."

INTO THE WOODS

The southern woods were dense and dark, the trees towering above like silent sentinels. Aria moved quietly, her claws extended and her senses sharp. The bond pulsed faintly in her chest, steadying her as she scanned the shadows for any sign of movement.

Hunter trailed a few steps behind, his golden eyes watchful. "You didn't have to agree so quickly," he said, his voice low.

"If I hadn't, they'd still think I'm weak," she replied, her tone clipped. "I don't need you second-guessing me."

"I'm not," he said evenly. "But this isn't just about proving yourself. It's about survival."

She stopped, turning to face him. "Then let me survive the way I know how."

For a moment, Hunter said nothing. Then he nodded, stepping back to give her space. "Just don't forget—we're in this together."

The bond pulsed stronger at his words, and Aria hated the way it steadied her. She turned away, focusing on the task ahead.

THE ROGUE SHADOW

The air grew colder as they moved deeper into the woods, the scent of damp earth and decay filling Aria's nose. Her wolf growled low, uneasy. She knew this feeling—the oppressive weight, the faint hum in the air. A shadow was near.

"There," Hunter said softly, his golden eyes fixed on a dark shape moving between the trees.

Aria followed his gaze, her claws twitching. The shadow was smaller than the ones they'd faced before, but its movements were erratic, its red eyes glowing faintly in the dark.

"Stay back," she said, her voice firm.

"Aria—"

"I mean it," she snapped, cutting him off. "This is my fight."

Hunter hesitated, his golden eyes narrowing, but he nodded. "Fine. But I'm not leaving."

She didn't respond. Her focus was locked on the shadow now, her wolf rising to the surface. The bond hummed faintly, but she shoved it aside. This was her chance to prove she didn't need it—or him.

She moved quickly, her claws slicing through the air as she lunged at the shadow. It screeched, its form twisting and coiling as it struck back. The fight was fast and brutal, the shadow's movements unpredictable. Aria's claws found their mark several times, but each strike seemed to make the creature more erratic, its red eyes glowing brighter.

Her breath came in sharp bursts, her muscles burning. The shadow lunged again, its tendrils aiming for her chest. She dodged, but not fast enough—a sharp pain seared through her side as one of the tendrils grazed her.

"Aria!" Hunter's voice cut through the chaos, but she didn't look back. Her wolf roared, her claws glowing faintly with golden light as she struck again. This time, the shadow let out a high-pitched shriek, its form unraveling before dissolving into smoke.

AFTERMATH

Aria stumbled back, her claws retracting as she pressed a hand to her side. The wound wasn't deep, but it throbbed painfully. Hunter was at her side in an instant, his golden eyes scanning her with concern.

"You're hurt," he said, his voice low.

"I'm fine," she muttered, brushing him off. "It's done."

Hunter didn't argue, but the tension in his jaw was clear. He stepped back, his gaze shifting to the empty space where the shadow had been. "They'll send more," he said quietly. "This was just a scout."

"I know," Aria said, her voice steady despite the pain. "But it was a start."

CHAPTER END

As they made their way back to the town, the bond pulsed faintly in Aria's chest. She hated how it steadied her, how it felt like a lifeline she didn't want to need. But for now, she would use it—because the fight was far from over.

When they reached the square, the alphas were waiting. Carrick's dark eyes swept over her, his smirk returning as he noticed the blood on her side.

"Well?" he asked, his tone dripping with amusement. "How was the hunt?"

Aria met his gaze, her voice cold and unyielding. "Successful."

CHAPTER 17

The Gathering Storm

The town square was alive with tension as Aria Bennett stepped into its center. The blood staining her side had dried, but the ache lingered, a sharp reminder of the fight. The alphas and their entourages watched her closely, their expressions a mix of skepticism and curiosity.

Hunter stood at her side, his golden eyes scanning the crowd. The bond between them pulsed faintly, steadying her despite her best efforts to ignore it.

Carrick, the broad-shouldered alpha, broke the silence. "You survived," he said, his tone amused. "Impressive."

"I didn't just survive," Aria said, her voice firm. **"I won."**

The murmurs among the shifters grew louder, the weight of her words rippling through the crowd. Aria's wolf bristled, uneasy under their scrutiny, but she held her ground.

Mara stepped forward, her sharp eyes gleaming. "A rogue shadow is one thing," she said. "But the Old Ones won't send scouts forever. What happens when the real fight begins?"

Aria clenched her fists, her claws twitching. "We fight," she said simply. "Together."

A DIVIDED COUNCIL

The alphas exchanged glances, their expressions ranging from wary to outright doubtful. Warrick, the dark-eyed alpha who had been quiet until now, finally spoke. "Fighting together sounds noble, but uniting packs is easier said than done. Each of us has our own lands, our own people to protect."

"Your lands won't matter if the Old Ones rise," Hunter said, his voice cold. "They'll take everything."

"And you expect us to follow her?" Warrick asked, his gaze settling on Aria. "A rogue omega with no pack?"

"She's more than that," Hunter said, stepping forward. "She's unbound. And she's proven herself stronger than any of you expected."

Aria felt the bond pulse again, a faint hum that steadied her as the alphas turned their attention to her. She took a deep breath, forcing herself to meet their gazes.

"I know you don't trust me," she said, her voice steady. "I wouldn't trust me either. But this isn't about me. It's about survival. The Old Ones aren't just coming for me—they're coming for all of us. And if we don't stand together, we're already lost."

THE FIRST STEP

The murmurs rose again, louder this time. Mara's sharp gaze flicked to Warrick, who nodded reluctantly. "Fine," Warrick said, his voice measured. "We'll stand with you. But unity won't come easily. You'll need to prove yourself—again and again."

"I'm used to it," Aria replied, her tone cold.

Carrick chuckled, stepping forward. "And what's your plan, rogue? How do you intend to stop the Old Ones?"

Aria glanced at Hunter, the bond pulsing faintly between them. "We start by preparing," she said. "Training, building alliances, and finding out what the Old Ones want. If we can understand them, we can stop them."

"You make it sound simple," Mara said, a faint smirk curling her lips. "But you've got fire, rogue. Let's see if it burns bright enough."

THE TRAINING BEGINS

The days that followed were grueling. The packs stayed in the town, their alphas watching as Aria and Hunter led training sessions in the square. Shifters sparred in pairs, their claws slicing through the air as they honed their skills.

Aria threw herself into the work, her body aching from the constant exertion. Her wolf snarled beneath the surface, restless but focused. Each strike of her claws felt sharper, more precise, as though the bond was guiding her movements.

"You're improving," Hunter said one evening, his tone neutral.

"Don't sound so surprised," Aria muttered, brushing dirt from her hands.

"I'm not," he said, his golden eyes meeting hers. "But this isn't enough."

She frowned, her claws retracting. "What do you mean?"

He stepped closer, lowering his voice. "The shadows we've faced are just the beginning. The Old Ones will send something stronger—something we've never seen before. And when they do, you'll need more than claws to survive."

Her stomach tightened at his words, but she forced herself to stand tall. "Then teach me."

AN OMINOUS MESSAGE

As night fell over the town, a new tension filled the air. The faint hum Aria had felt before battles returned, sharper now. Her wolf growled softly, its unease prickling along her skin.

"Do you feel that?" she asked, turning to Hunter.

He nodded, his golden eyes narrowing. "Something's coming."

Before she could respond, a high-pitched screech cut through the night. Shifters poured into the square, their claws extended as they scanned the darkened streets. The sound came again, closer this time, and Aria's blood ran cold.

A shadow appeared at the edge of the square—not like the ones they had fought before. This one was larger, its form more defined. Its red eyes blazed as it stepped forward, its movements deliberate.

"Is that—" Aria began, but Hunter cut her off.

"It's not alone," he said grimly.

More shadows emerged from the darkness, their forms coiling and twisting unnaturally. The shifters around them braced themselves, their claws glowing faintly with energy.

The lead shadow stopped suddenly, its red eyes locking onto Aria. When it spoke, its voice was layered and cold, vibrating through the air like a living thing.

"She belongs to us."

CHAPTER END

The square erupted into chaos as the shadows surged forward, their screeches cutting through the night. Aria's claws extended, the bond pulsing stronger now, as she prepared to fight.

The storm had arrived.

CHAPTER 18

Shadows Unleashed

The shadows surged forward, their red eyes blazing ... the dark. The square erupted into ... moved to intercept them, their ... with energy. Aria Bennett stood at ... ... nding as she braced herself for the

Hunter's voice cut through the noise, sharp and commanding. "Hold the line!"

The packs responded instantly, their movements fluid as they formed a loose perimeter around the square. Aria's claws extended, the bond pulsing faintly in her chest as her wolf pushed forward. This wasn't a sparring match. This was survival.

A BATTLE OF INSTINCTS

The first shadow lunged at her, its form coiling and twisting unnaturally. Aria dodged, her claws slashing through its side. The creature shrieked, its body unraveling briefly before reforming. Her wolf growled, the bond humming louder as she moved faster, more precisely.

"You can't fight them alone!" Hunter shouted, appearing at her side. His claws glowed with golden energy as he struck another shadow, the light cutting through its form like a blade. "Stay with me."

Aria bit back a retort, focusing instead on the shadow in front of her. It lunged again, its tendrils snapping like whips, but this time she was ready. She met its strike head-on, her claws glowing faintly as they sliced through the dark energy. The creature shrieked and dissolved, its eyes flickering out.

More shadows poured into the square, their m faster, more coordinated. Aria and Hunter m their strikes synchronized as the bond pulsed stronger, guiding them like a single force.

THE PACK'S STRENGTH

Around the square, the packs fought with a ferocity that surprised even Aria. Mara moved like a blur, her claws tearing through shadows with precision. Warrick and Carrick led their packmates in coordinated strikes, their movements fluid and relentless.

For the first time, Aria saw the potential in their unity. Despite their differences, the packs fought as one, their combined strength pushing the shadows back.

But the fight was far from over.

THE LEAD SHADOW

The lead shadow, larger and more defined than the others, moved with chilling deliberation. Its red eyes locked onto Aria, its form coiling like smoke as it advanced. The other shadows seemed to respond to it, their movements growing more aggressive, more focused.

"It's targeting you," Hunter said, his voice grim. "Stay close."

Aria clenched her fists, her claws twitching. "I don't need you protecting me."

"This isn't about you," he snapped, his golden eyes blazing. "If it gets to you, we all lose."

The bond pulsed sharply, almost like a warning. Aria's wolf snarled, its energy surging as the lead shadow lunged. She moved instinctively, her claws glowing brighter as they met its strike.

The impact sent a shockwave through the square, forcing several shifters to stumble. The lead shadow recoiled, its form flickering, but it didn't dissolve. Instead, it shifted, splitting into multiple tendrils that struck out in all directions.

Hunter stepped in front of her, his claws slashing through the tendrils with precision. "Stay focused," he said, his voice steady. "The bond will guide you."

Aria hated how much she needed his words, but she let the bond hum louder, steadying her movements as she struck again. The lead shadow screeched, its form unraveling slightly, but it didn't fall.

A NEW SURGE

The tide seemed to shift as the shadows pressed harder, their attacks growing more frantic. Aria's muscles burned, her breath coming in sharp bursts, but she refused to falter.

Around her, the shifters fought valiantly, but the strain was clear.

"They're not letting up!" Mara shouted, her voice cutting through the noise.

Warrick cursed under his breath, his claws glowing faintly. "We can't hold them off forever."

Aria's wolf growled, its frustration matching her own. The bond pulsed stronger now, almost painfully, as though urging her to act. She didn't know how, but she felt the energy building inside her, a fire that threatened to consume her.

The lead shadow lunged again, its form twisting unnaturally as it aimed for her chest. Aria moved faster than she thought possible, her claws glowing brilliantly as they met its strike. The golden light flared, blindingly bright, as the shadow screeched and dissolved completely.

The other shadows froze briefly, their red eyes flickering as though disoriented. The shifters seized the opportunity, striking hard and fast, their claws cutting through the remaining creatures. One by one, the shadows fell, their forms unraveling into smoke.

AFTERMATH

The square was eerily silent as the last shadow dissolved, leaving only the faint hum of the bond in Aria's chest. Her claws retracted as she stumbled back, her legs trembling with exhaustion. Hunter was at her side in an instant, his golden eyes scanning her for injuries.

"You're hurt," he said, his voice low.

"I'm fine," she muttered, though her body ached in ways she hadn't expected. She glanced around the square, her gaze sweeping over the shifters. They were battered but standing, their expressions a mix of relief and disbelief.

Carrick stepped forward, his dark eyes narrowing as he looked at Aria. "That light," he said, his tone cautious. "What was that?"

Aria hesitated, her stomach twisting. She didn't have an answer, but the bond pulsed faintly, steadying her. "I don't know," she admitted. "But it worked."

THE ALPHA'S VERDICT

Mara smirked faintly, brushing dirt from her hands. "You've got more in you than I thought, rogue."

Warrick nodded, his expression grudgingly respectful. "That fight bought you some time. But the Old Ones won't stop. This was just a taste of what's coming."

"I know," Aria said, her voice steady despite the exhaustion. "And we'll be ready."

Hunter's golden eyes met hers, a faint flicker of approval in his gaze. "You're stronger than you realize," he said quietly. "But strength alone won't win this war."

"Then teach me," Aria replied, her voice firm. "Because I'm not running anymore."

CHAPTER END

As the first light of dawn broke over the horizon, Aria stood in the square, her body aching but her resolve stronger than ever. The bond pulsed faintly in her chest, a steady reminder of the fight ahead.

The storm wasn't over. It was just beginning.

CHAPTER 19

Strength in Unity

The morning light washed over the town, casting long shadows across the square where the remnants of the battle lingered. The air was heavy with exhaustion and the faint, acrid scent of dissipated shadows. Shifters moved quietly, tending to wounds and gathering their strength. The fight was over, but the tension hadn't eased.

Aria Bennett stood near the center of the square, her body aching from the battle. Her wolf was restless, pacing beneath her skin as if sensing that the victory was only temporary. The bond pulsed faintly in her chest, steady and persistent, a reminder that the storm wasn't over.

Hunter approached, his golden eyes scanning her carefully. "You held your ground."

"And so did they," Aria replied, nodding toward the shifters. "They're stronger than I thought."

"They'll need to be," Hunter said, his tone grim. "The Old Ones won't stop sending scouts. This was a test, and we've just barely passed."

A FRAGILE ALLIANCE

The alphas gathered in the small hall; their expressions guarded as they sat around the rough-hewn table. Carrick leaned back in his chair, his dark eyes fixed on Aria with a mix of curiosity and wariness. Mara stood near the wall, her sharp gaze flicking between the others. Warrick, ever the strategist, spoke first.

"The shadows are getting stronger," he said, his voice measured. "If that was just a scout, we're in deeper trouble than we thought."

"And you think this rogue is the answer?" Carrick asked, his tone sceptical. "She's powerful, sure, but power isn't enough to lead a war."

Aria's jaw tightened, her wolf bristling at his words. "I'm not trying to lead your war. I'm trying to survive it."

"And you think we're not?" Mara said, her tone sharp. "Every pack here has something to lose. We're not risking everything on blind faith."

Hunter stepped forward, his golden eyes blazing. "This isn't about faith. It's about survival. The Old Ones don't care about your borders or your pack politics. They'll take everything unless we stand together."

The room fell silent, the weight of his words pressing down on them. Warrick leaned forward, his dark eyes thoughtful. "If we're going to do this, we need more than strength. We need a plan."

THE PLAN FORMS

Hunter nodded, his tone firm. "We start by fortifying the town. The shadows are drawn to Aria, and if they come again, we need to be ready."

"And what happens when they send something stronger?" Mara asked, her claws tapping against the table.

"We'll adapt," Hunter said. "But we can't fight this war alone. We need to bring more packs into the alliance."

Carrick scoffed. "Good luck with that. Most alphas won't leave their territories, let alone risk their packs for a cause they don't believe in."

"Then we make them believe," Aria said, her voice steady. The bond pulsed faintly in her chest, lending her strength. "We show them the threat is real. If they won't come to us, we go to them."

The alphas exchanged glances; their scepticism evident. But Warrick nodded slowly. "It's a risk," he said. "But it's the only way. If the Old Ones are moving, we need to move faster."

PREPARING FOR THE JOURNEY

The town buzzed with activity as preparations began. Supplies were gathered, weapons sharpened, and defenses reinforced. Aria threw herself into the work, her muscles protesting with every movement but her wolf urging her forward.

Hunter watched her closely, his golden eyes unreadable. "You're pushing yourself too hard."

"I don't have a choice," she replied, brushing dirt from her hands. "If we wait, we lose."

"You won't help anyone if you collapse," he said, his tone softer now. "Take a moment to breathe."

Aria hesitated, the bond pulsing faintly. She hated how his words steadied her, how the bond made her feel like she wasn't alone. But she nodded reluctantly, stepping away to catch her breath.

A MOMENT OF REFLECTION

That evening, Aria sat on the ridge overlooking the town. The distant glow of the pack lands shimmered on the horizon, a faint reminder of what was at stake. Her wolf was quiet now, watching, waiting.

Hunter joined her, his presence steady but not overbearing. For a while, they sat in silence, the bond humming faintly between them.

"You were right," Aria said finally, her voice low. "I can't do this alone."

Hunter's golden eyes softened slightly. "You're not alone. The packs may be slow to trust, but they're here. And so am I."

She glanced at him, her jaw tightening. "I still don't trust you."

"You don't have to," he said simply. "But you trust the bond."

She didn't respond, but the bond pulsed again, stronger now. It wasn't trust—not yet—but it was enough.

THE ROAD AHEAD

By dawn, the small group was ready. Hunter and Aria led the way, flanked by Mara and Warrick. The other packs remained behind to defend the town, their gazes wary but determined as they watched the group depart.

The journey to the first pack's territory was quiet, the forest dense and alive with the sounds of wildlife. Aria's wolf was alert, every shadow and rustling leaf making her tense. The bond hummed faintly, a steady reminder of Hunter's presence.

"What do you know about this pack?" she asked, breaking the silence.

"They're strong," Hunter said. "But cautious. Their alpha won't join easily."

"Great," Aria muttered. "More tests."

Hunter smirked faintly. "Consider it practice."

CHAPTER END

As they reached the edge of the pack's territory, the air grew heavier, the faint hum of energy making Aria's wolf growl softly. Hunter's golden eyes narrowed as he scanned the treeline.

"They know we're here," he said quietly.

Aria clenched her fists, her claws extending. The bond pulsed, steady and strong.

The storm was far from over.

CHAPTER 20

The Edge of Neutrality

The forest loomed around them, its dense canopy blocking out most of the morning light. Aria Bennett moved silently; her senses sharp as she scanned the shadows between the trees. Her wolf was restless, its low growl vibrating faintly in her chest. The bond pulsed steadily, a reminder of Hunter's presence just behind her.

"They've known we were coming since we crossed the ridge," Hunter said quietly, his golden eyes scanning the treeline. "They'll be watching."

Aria glanced back at him, her claws twitching at her sides. "Then let's give them something to watch."

Warrick snorted softly, his dark eyes glinting with amusement. "Bold. I'll give you that."

Mara, walking beside him, smirked faintly. "Let's hope bold doesn't get us killed."

The group moved carefully, their movements deliberate as they entered the pack's territory. The air was thick with tension, the faint hum of energy pressing down on them. Aria's wolf bristled, its unease mirroring her own.

A CAUTIOUS WELCOME

They emerged into a clearing, the forest opening up to reveal a wide expanse of land bordered by jagged cliffs. At its center stood a gathering of shifters, their postures rigid as they watched the newcomers approach. Their alpha, a tall woman with sharp features and piercing gray eyes, stood at the forefront.

"So," the alpha said, her voice cool and commanding. "This is the rogue everyone's been whispering about."

Aria stepped forward, her claws retracting as she met the alpha's gaze. "Aria Bennett. And you are?"

The woman's lips twitched into a faint smirk. "Lucia. Alpha of the Silver Fang pack. And you're bold, I'll give you that."

Aria crossed her arms, her wolf growling softly. "Bold's gotten me this far."

Lucia chuckled, a low, humorless sound. "Has it? We'll see."

THE TEST OF FAITH

Lucia's gaze swept over the group, lingering briefly on Hunter. "And you brought the Golden Fang's heir. Interesting. I thought you'd abandoned diplomacy."

Hunter's golden eyes narrowed slightly. "This isn't about diplomacy. It's about survival."

Lucia's expression darkened, her claws extending faintly. "Survival means nothing without strength. And I don't gamble on weakness."

Aria bristled, her wolf snapping beneath her skin. "I'm not weak."

Lucia tilted her head, studying her. "Prove it."

The words hung in the air, heavy and deliberate. Aria stepped forward, her claws extending as she met Lucia's gaze head-on. "What do you want?"

"A challenge," Lucia said, her tone cold. "Not just strength. Instinct. Adaptability. You'll face three trials, and if you survive, we'll talk."

Hunter stepped forward, his posture tense. "This isn't necessary—"

"It is," Lucia interrupted, her gray eyes sharp. "If she wants my trust, she'll earn it."

TRIAL ONE: THE GAUNTLET

The first trial began almost immediately. Aria was led to a narrow canyon lined with jagged rocks and twisted roots. The Silver Fang shifters watched silently from the edges, their expressions unreadable.

Lucia stood at the entrance, her voice low but firm. "This is the Gauntlet. Make it through without faltering, and you'll pass."

Aria clenched her fists, her claws twitching. "What's the catch?"

Lucia smirked faintly. "You'll see."

As Aria stepped into the canyon, the air grew colder, the shadows deeper. Her wolf growled softly, its unease prickling along her skin. The bond pulsed faintly, steadying her as she moved forward.

The first attack came quickly—a sudden surge of movement from the shadows. A Silver Fang shifter lunged at her, their claws slicing through the air. Aria dodged instinctively, her claws extending as she countered. The clash was brief but brutal, her strikes precise as she forced the shifter back.

More attacks followed, each one faster and more calculated than the last. Aria's muscles burned as she moved, her wolf lending her strength. The bond pulsed louder now, guiding her movements as she struck with precision.

By the time she reached the end of the canyon, her breath was ragged, her body aching. But she was standing, and the shifters who had tested her watched with grudging respect.

Lucia waited at the exit, her expression unreadable. "Not bad, rogue. But this was the easy part."

TRIAL TWO: THE PACK'S JUDGMENT

The second trial was less physical but no less grueling. Aria was brought to a circle of Silver Fang shifters, their eyes cold and assessing. Lucia stood at the center, her posture rigid.

"This is the Pack's Judgment," Lucia said. "They'll decide if you're worthy of our alliance."

Aria clenched her fists, her wolf growling softly. "And how do I prove that?"

"By convincing them," Lucia replied. "Words, actions — it doesn't matter. But you have to make them believe."

The shifters circled her, their questions sharp and unrelenting. They challenged her strength, her motives, her ability to lead. Each word was a test, each glare a challenge.

Aria's voice remained steady, her answers firm but honest. She spoke of the shadows, the Old Ones, and the battles she'd faced. She didn't sugarcoat the truth or hide her fears. Instead, she let them see her determination, her refusal to back down.

When the questioning ended, the shifters stepped back, their gazes wary but no longer hostile. Lucia nodded, a faint flicker of approval in her gray eyes. "You're not as reckless as you seem."

CHAPTER END

As Aria prepared for the final trial, the air grew heavier, the faint hum of energy pressing down on her chest. The bond pulsed louder now, steady and strong, as if bracing her for what was to come.

Lucia stepped forward, her expression cold. "The last trial is simple. Face your fears. Survive, and you'll have my trust."

Aria's wolf growled, its energy surging as she nodded. "Bring it on."

The storm wasn't over yet.

CHAPTER 21

The Final Trial

The forest around Aria Bennett was unnaturally quiet as she stepped into the heart of Silver Fang territory. The air was heavy, almost suffocating, and the faint hum of energy prickled along her skin. Her wolf bristled, uneasy but alert.

Lucia stood at the edge of the clearing, her sharp gray eyes fixed on Aria. "This trial isn't about strength or clever words," she said, her tone cold. "It's about facing what's inside you. Your fears. Your doubts. Your failures."

Aria's claws twitched, her wolf growling softly. "And if I don't?"

"Then you're not ready to lead," Lucia said bluntly. "And you're not worth following."

Hunter stepped closer, his golden eyes steady as he met Aria's gaze. The bond between them pulsed faintly, a steady rhythm that felt both grounding and unnerving. "You've already faced worse," he said quietly. "This is just another fight."

Aria swallowed hard, her jaw tightening. She didn't respond, but she nodded once, stepping into the clearing. The energy thickened immediately, the air buzzing with an almost electric charge. Her wolf growled louder, its unease mirroring her own.

THE TRIAL BEGINS

As Aria reached the center of the clearing, the world seemed to shift. The trees blurred, their shapes distorting until they disappeared completely. She was standing in darkness now, the air cold and oppressive. Her wolf snarled, but even its presence felt muted.

Then she heard it—a faint whisper, barely audible but unmistakable. Her own voice.

"You're not strong enough."

The words cut through her like a blade, sharper than she expected. She turned sharply, her claws extending, but there was no one there. Only the darkness and the sound of her own heartbeat.

"You'll fail them. Just like you always do."

Her breath hitched, her wolf snapping at her chest. "Shut up," she muttered, her voice shaking. "This isn't real."

But the whispers grew louder, swirling around her like a storm. Images began to flicker in the darkness—her parents' disapproving faces, the looks of mistrust from the alphas, the shadows' glowing red eyes. Each one was sharper, more vivid than the last.

"You can't save them."

"You're just a rogue. A failure."

"You're not enough."

FACING THE SHADOW

The whispers coalesced suddenly, forming a shape in the darkness. Aria froze as a figure stepped forward—herself, but different. This version of her had glowing red eyes, her claws dripping with dark energy. Her shadow-self smirked, its voice cold and mocking.

"You think you're a leader?" the shadow hissed. "You're nothing but prey. A scared little girl pretending to be strong."

Aria's wolf snarled, its energy surging as she extended her claws. "You're not real."

The shadow laughed, a low, chilling sound. "Oh, I'm very real. I'm every failure, every weakness, every fear you've ever had. And I'm stronger than you."

The shadow lunged, its claws slicing through the air. Aria moved instinctively, her own claws meeting the strike with a sharp crack. The impact sent a shockwave through the darkness, the force of it making her stumble.

The fight was brutal, each strike forcing Aria to confront her own insecurities. The shadow's taunts cut deeper than its claws, its words echoing in her mind even as she struck back.

"You'll never be enough."

"They don't trust you. They never will."

"You'll fail them."

The bond pulsed sharply in her chest, a steady hum that drowned out the whispers. Aria gritted her teeth, her claws glowing faintly with golden light as she struck again, her voice steady. "You're wrong."

The shadow reeled, its form flickering. Aria pressed forward, her strikes faster, more precise. The bond burned brighter now, a fire in her veins that steadied her when her strength wavered.

"I'm not perfect," she said, her voice rising. "But I'm not weak. And I'm not afraid of you."

With a final, blinding strike, the shadow dissolved, its red eyes flickering out as the darkness shattered around her.

EMERGING FROM THE TRIAL

Aria stumbled back into the clearing, her breath ragged and her body trembling. The oppressive energy was gone, replaced by the soft rustle of the forest and the faint warmth of the morning sun.

Lucia was waiting at the edge, her gray eyes sharp but unreadable. "Well?"

Aria straightened, forcing herself to meet the alpha's gaze. "It's done."

Lucia studied her for a moment, then nodded. "You've faced yourself and survived. That's more than most can say."

Hunter stepped forward, his golden eyes scanning her carefully. "You did it."

Aria nodded, the bond pulsing faintly in her chest. For the first time, she didn't push it away. "Yeah. I did."

THE PACK'S DECISION

That evening, the Silver Fang pack gathered in the main hall. The air was heavy with anticipation as Lucia stepped forward, her posture commanding.

"The rogue has proven herself," Lucia said, her voice carrying through the room. "She's faced our trials and earned my trust."

The murmurs that followed were less skeptical this time, the tension in the room shifting. Warrick and Mara exchanged glances; their expressions thoughtful.

"You've got my pack," Lucia said, her gray eyes locking onto Aria. "But don't waste it."

Aria nodded; her voice steady. "I won't."

CHAPTER END

As the group prepared to leave Silver Fang territory, Aria stood at the edge of the clearing, her gaze fixed on the distant horizon. The bond pulsed steadily in her chest, a reminder of the fight ahead.

Hunter stepped up beside her, his golden eyes warm. "The hardest part is over."

Aria smirked faintly, her claws twitching. "Not even close."

The storm was growing, and this time, she was ready.

9 798348 232573